Caught in a Blizzard

The snowflakes hitting the window of Susan's car were growing larger and wetter by the minute.

Damn it, she thought to herself, if we had only started a couple of hours earlier we would've made it home and wouldn't be out in this mess.

Nervously glancing over at her son, she saw that he too was watching the snow as it swirled around the car.

Turning her attention back to the road, she concentrated on keeping the car between the disappearing lane markers.

"Mom, it sure is snowing hard," Danny said, nervously looking over at her.

"I know, Honey" she returned, trying to keep the concern out of her voice "I wish we had started out a couple of hours earlier and we would be back home by now."

"Are you going to try to make it home tonight?" he asked, "It's really getting bad."

"I don't think we'll be able to make it home," she sighed, feeling the wheels spin precariously on the thickening snow, "I think we are going to have to find a motel and spend the night."

"I think that's a good idea," he exhaled loudly, "it's starting to get scary out here."

"Start looking for a place we can get some groceries, so we can eat in the room," she told him, concentrating on keeping the car on the road, "I don't think we're going to find any cafes open in this storm."

Peering out the snow encrusted window, Danny occasionally glanced over at his mother who drove along with a white-knuckled grip on the steering wheel.

Finally, in the snow-blurred distance, he saw the lights of a mini-mart.

"Look, Mom, I think there's a store-mart right up there," he said, pointing up ahead.

"Thank goodness," she groaned, "this road is really getting slick."

Gratefully guiding the car into the parking lot, through the slippery snow, she slowed down and let it come to sliding stop directly in front of the doors.

"We made it," she gushed, setting the emergency brake, and turning the engine off. "Hurry up and pick out what you want. I'll be in, in a minute."

"Okay," Danny said, opening the door and stepping out into the wind-whipped snow.

"Hurry," she called out to him as she looked for her purse, "so we can find a motel before it gets any worse."

Finding her purse, she grabbed it and paused for a second to watch her eighteen-year-old son dash into the mart. She was glad he was with her. Just having him along made her feel safer.

He was a good boy, she smiled to herself. He had turned out much better than she had ever hoped as she had raised him all by herself since his father's death six years earlier.

Putting her thoughts about him aside for a few moments, she reached into the back seat and got her jacket. It wasn't very substantial, but it would keep the cold out for the short dash into the store and back. She had slipped her shoes off to drive, but now she was wishing she hadn't worn heels. They would make walking in the snow treacherous, but she had to wear something or freeze her feet off. Quickly slipping her jacket on, she pulled it around her tightly and stepped out into the cold. She could feel the giant, white snowflakes wetly blowing into her face as she slipped out and clomped through the snow to the door.

Stepping inside, she brushed the snow off her jacket as she looked around. Smiling, she saw that Danny had a pile of goodies on the counter waiting for her. Hurrying over to the shelves, she gathered up a few more things, including a big bottle of Rhine wine and set it all on the counter beside Danny's pile.

"Might as well make the most of it," she smiled at the clerk as he rang up their groceries.

"It sure is a mess out there tonight," the attendant said as he sacked up their groceries.

"It sure is," Susan responded. "Do you know of any motels that might have a vacancy tonight?"

"Well, Ma'am, I really don't know," he told her, taking her money, "this storm probably has most of them full, by now. But there's one out at the edge of town. They usually have vacancies, but I don't know on a night like tonight. I was just about to close up myself before y'all came in."

"I sure hope they do," she said, taking her change.

"Good luck," he said, watching them pick up the sacks and head for the door.

"It looks like we'll need it," she said over her shoulder as she stepped out the door.

Sliding along the snow-slickened sidewalk, Susan stepped down off the curb and felt her foot start to slide out from under her.

"Whoops," she yelped as she started to fall.

But before she could fall, Danny reached out and caught her. Wrapping one arm around her, he pulled her to him as he struggled not to drop his bag of groceries. As he did, he suddenly found his hand filled with the soft fullness of his mother's breast. There was nothing he could do but hold on to keep her from falling.

"Gosh, Mom," he admonished her as he stood holding her pressed up against him as she regained her balance, "you'd better be careful."

"Thanks for catching me," she smiled at him.

"You're welcome," he blushed, feeling the softness of his mother's breast in his hand and her soft, warm body pressed up against him.

"Can you make it the rest of the way?" he asked her, finally stepping back away from her.

"I think so," she said, reaching over and steadying herself by holding onto the car.

Danny just stood there watching her struggle down the car. Finally, she had her door open and went sliding into the car as Danny watched on.

Just as he started to turn and walk around the car, he saw his mother's dress ride up her creamy white thigh. Riding higher and higher, it went all the way up until he could see the lacy bottom of her panties, revealing all of her long, shapely leg.

Rudely gawking at her, he watched her shove her dress back down and slam the door shut.

Feeling guilty for some strange reason, he felt his face growing warm in embarrassment. If it had been any other woman, he would have gotten a real rush at seeing so much exposed flesh, but it was his mother. But why then, he asked himself as he stumbled around the car, why had he felt a rush of excitement? Well, she did have beautiful legs. That had to be it. Had to be, because he couldn't even think of his mother in that way.

"I'm glad I'm not a girl," he said to her as he slid into the car, trying to make light of it.

"And why is that?" his mother asked, slipping off her shoes.

"Wearing high heels in weather like this is dangerous," he said, glad that his mother couldn't see him blushing in the darkness of the car.

"They sure are," she laughed, sticking the key in the ignition. "I was a real dumb ass for wearing them."

"You look nice in them," he said softly.

"Why, thank you," she said, looking over at him briefly.

Turning back around, she started the car and slowly drove across the parking lot.

"Well, here goes," she complained as she pulled back out onto the empty highway.

As they drove through town, they peered out through the snow-packed windows searching for a motel with a vacancy. It was getting harder to see out through the thickening snow storm, and all they found were motels with "NO VACANCY" signs displayed out front.

Finally, at the very edge of town, a blinking "VACANCY" sign caught their eyes.

"Yippee," she yipped, guiding the car off the slippery highway.

"You got that right," Danny grinned, watching his mother maneuver the car through the deepening snow up to the motel entrance.

"Whew," she gushed, stopping the car. "I'm glad we made it."

"Me too," he said, looking over at the motel door, almost obscured by the drifting snow.

"I'll go in and register," she told Danny.

"Be careful," he told her, "and don't fall this time."

"I'll try not to," she laughed, sliding out of the car.

Danny watched as she clumsily clopped through the snow, slipping and sliding, but not falling as she made her way up to the door.

Sitting there waiting for her, he thought back to the incident in the mini-mart parking lot. His face warmed with embarrassment again as he remembered the feel of her breast in his hand. It wasn't like he had grabbed hold of her breast while she was naked or anything, he told himself. He could feel the texture of her brassiere through her jacket and blouse, but just the feel of her big, soft breast in his hand was enough to make him all warm inside. Then, when he had seen his mother's bare leg, it had only complicated things. He knew that it was an accident. But, it still disturbed him. He had seen his mother's legs before, but there was something disquieting about it this time.

Maybe it was the double whammy of her breast and her leg at the same time. Anyway, it gave him the shakes. It had excited him and that was what was scary. He had gotten a sick thrill out of it. Jeez, he complained to himself. What kind of pervert was he anyway? Thinking that way about his mother.

Trying to think about something else. Anything else but that, he watched the snow coming down harder and harder. They were really lucky to find a motel before it got any worse, he thought.

Were they going to have to stay in the same room? Of, course they would, but they would each have a bed of their own. Still, it would feel funny, sleeping in the same room as his mother. But, what the hell, they were lucky to get anything with the weather like it was.

Looking back out at the highway, he saw the snow covering the road was getting deeper by the second.

Then he realized how hungry he was. He wished his mother would hurry so they could eat. Digging into one of the bags, he started to pull out a bag of chips when he saw his mother push out through the door.

As she trudged back toward the car, Danny slid over and opened her door for her.

"Whew, it's nasty out here," she complained, stretching her leg inside and sliding underneath the steering wheel.

Shamefully, Danny couldn't keep from looking down at her legs as he watched her dress ride up again. But this time, she caught it with her hand before it had gotten much more than six inches above her knee.

"Did we get a room?" he asked her.

"Yep. But the owner said we needed to be prepared for anything with a storm like this," she laughed uneasily.

"Oh," Danny gulped. "Like what?"

"I don't know," she said, "I didn't ask him. I was just happy to get a room. His last one."

"We were lucky," Danny grinned.

"Hey, we've got a room and food and some wine. We'll just pretend that we're on a picnic and have a party. Okay?"

"Sure, Mom," Danny laughed half-heartedly. "A picnic in a blizzard."

She started the car and carefully guided it around the parking lot to the space in front of their room. "This is the last room he had," she said repeating herself as she turned off the engine, "we were really lucky to get it."

They hurriedly gathered up their things and stepped out of the car.

"At least we got one," Danny said as they went clomping through the snow carrying their suitcases and the sack of food up to the door of their room.

"You can say that again," she said opening the door of their room and stepping inside.

Danny stepped in right behind her and looked around.

"Uh, Mom, there's only one bed," he said, blushing.

"I know, Honey" she said, "But, it was the only room he had."

"Brrrrr, it sure is cold in here," he whined.

"It's like ice in here," she mumbled, hurrying over to the thermostat and turning it up to the maximum.

"I hope the heater works."

"You'd better believe it," he said, breathing out and seeing his breath in the frigid air of the room, "if it doesn't, we'll freeze to death."

As he spoke, they heard the heating unit click on and felt a rush of warm air gush into the room from the heating duct.

"Thank goodness," she laughed.

"I'll bet you're hungry," she chirped. "I'm starved."

"You'd better believe it," he groaned, rubbing his belly, "my stomach thinks that my throat's been cut."

"That's a good one," she laughed out loud.

Bringing over a couple of glasses from the bathroom, she sat them down on the coffee table and filled them with wine.

"Cheers," she said, lifting her glass and taking a big gulp of the wine.

"Good stuff," Danny said, following her example.

Sitting on the floor, using the coffee table as their table, they spread out their feast and began to eat. As they were eating, the air in the room gradually became warmer and warmer until at last, when temperature inside of the room had reached a comfortable warmness, the heater shut off.

"I feel a lot better, now," Susan told him as she leaned back and yawned, "do you?"

"I sure do," he yawned back at her, "what more could we ask for. A jug of wine, a loaf of bread and each other and we're not out on the highway fighting the storm."

"You've got that right," she mumbled, getting up and walking over to the windows.

Danny watched, admiring the soft roundness of her hips as they swayed back and forth under the thin material of her skirt.

Pulling the curtain back, she looked out at the swirling snow. It was snowing so hard, she could barely see their car that was only twenty or thirty feet away.

"For goodness sakes," she proclaimed in amazement, "it is snowing so hard, you can barely see our car."

"Really?" Danny mumbled, getting up and joining her at the window, "Wow, you're right. I don't think I've ever seen it snow so hard before."

Feeling happy and buoyed by the wine, he casually eased her hand around his mother's waist as they stared out into the dark.

Glancing over at him briefly, she smiled and turned back to the storm.

"I hope that we can get out of here tomorrow," she said apprehensively.

"Yeah, but we won't if it keeps snowing like this," he said, pulling her against him ever so slightly.

As they stood watching the blizzard for a few minutes, Danny thought he felt her relax slightly and lean against him.

It felt good to have her warm softness pressed up against him, he thought. Happily, he gave her a little squeeze and a kiss on the cheek.

"I love you, mom," he grinned down at her.

"Uh, I love you, too," she smiled back at him, "but I think that I'm going to take a shower and get ready for bed.

"It's been a very long day and I'm tired," she said, stepping out of his hold and walking over to her suitcase.

"Okay," he said, watching her rummage through her suitcase. "I'll wait until you're done."

"I would hope so," she laughed, refilling her wineglass and picking up her clothes, "I won't be too long."

"Take your time," he laughed softly, "I don't think I'll be going anywhere."

"Silly Boy," she chuckled as she disappeared into the bathroom.

Turning on the television, Danny sat on the edge of the bed next to her suitcase sipping on his wine, waiting for the television to warm up.

Just then he heard the shower come on.

Suddenly, he had the weirdest feeling come over him as he sat staring at the television. He had never felt such an utter sense of isolation before. It was as if he and his mother were the only people in the motel. Alone and stranded in the storm. A sudden sense of claustrophobia closed around him.

But it only lasted a few moments. Until he took another long swig of wine. Refilling his glass, he found himself thinking of his mother and the newly awakened feelings about her.

Then as he recalled the parking lot incident, he realized that she was standing no more than twenty feet away from him. Naked!

Why hadn't he had these feeling before? He and his mother had lived alone since he was eleven. That was when his father had been killed.

All that time and nothing like this had ever happened. They were as close as a boy and his mother could be, he thought. But why was he suddenly thinking about her as a woman? A sexual, sensual woman with breasts and legs, and . . . no, he couldn't say that word. She was his mother.

Suddenly; he found himself wondering what she looked like naked. Ashamed of himself, he still couldn't keep from imagining how beautiful she would be as she stood under the shower with the water running down her body. Running down over her big, round breasts, dripping off her nipples, coursing down over her belly, down between her legs to her secret place. Between her legs and over the softness hidden there. Oh, God, he groaned to himself, stop it.

Then to his horror and disgust, he realized that he was so hard it was beginning to ache.

Hating himself for his vile thoughts on the one hand, he found himself wanting to sneak over and see if he could peek into the bathroom and see her naked.

Berating himself for his sinfulness, he found himself staring down into his mother's open suitcase.

Hearing the shower still running, he curiously poked through her clothes. What was he doing? He couldn't believe what he was doing. He had never done anything like this before. In fact, he had never even thought of doing anything so grotesque before. Then he felt his fingers brush over something soft and silky.

It was a pair of sheer, dainty panties.

He felt his penis lurch with excitement as he timidly lifted the lacy panties out of her suitcase.

He felt his heart skip a beat as he looked down at the scanty fluff of material. My God, he thought, slipping his hand down inside her panties, you can see right through them.

Gawking down at his hand inside the gauzy panties, he knew that if his mother were wearing them, he would be able to see everything through the gossamer material.

Suddenly, the shower stopped and the panties became so hot, they were burning his fingers. Wanting to hide the vileness of his thoughts, he stuffed them down inside her suitcase and slammed it shut.

Jumping up, he stumbled over to the television and tried to make it look as if he were watching it as he waited for his mother to come back into the room.

Inside the shower, Susan reached down and turned the water off. It felt good to get her brassiere off, she thought, rubbing her big, pendulous breasts. She was so afraid that Danny would notice them as he had been growing up, she tried to keep them hidden inside of the tightest brassieres she could find.

Why she had done that, she couldn't really explain. But once she had started, she had just kept it up. Now here he was all grown up and she was still trying to hide them from him. What had he thought, she wondered, when he had grabbed a handful of her breast back at the store?

And she had seen the way he gawked at her when her skirt had ridden up her leg. Then, the unfamiliar intimacy, she had felt when he had put his hand around her waist. All this, coming so suddenly left her perplexed.

And now they were confined together in the small, claustrophobic tightness of a motel room. Although they had lived together, alone for six years, they had never been forced to share such limited space under such trying conditions.

And they had never had to share the same bed.

Looking into the mirror, she saw that she was blushing.

What was happening to her, she asked herself, taking another drink of her wine? She knew that she didn't have a choice about sharing a bed with him. She also knew that it shouldn't bother her, but she couldn't help feeling the least bit self-conscious about sleeping with her son.

SLEEPING WITH HER SON?

It sounded so obscene. Sleeping with her son. Why? That was exactly what they would be doing. Sleeping and nothing else.

How could you even be thinking such horrid things, she admonished herself as she ran the towel over her body.

Shaking, she folded the towel and laid it down on the counter.

Thank goodness, I brought my flannel gown, she told herself. It is so thick and concealing, she thought as she let it slide down her body covering her feminine curves from view.

But even as she was bewildered by the unnatural thoughts she was having about her and Danny, she was pleased with the way her body looked. She felt she was quite well maintained for her thirty-five years.

Glancing down she saw that while her gown masked most of her femininity, it couldn't hide the obvious swell of her imposing breasts as they jutted out conspicuously. Looking at herself in the mirror, she saw that every time she moved, it was easy to discern every little wiggle or jiggle of her breasts under the gown. Or was it just her imagination? Should she put her brassiere back on?

No, I won't do it, she told herself. I've been wearing that choking monstrosity all day long. Danny would just have to get used to the fact that his mother had breasts, she told herself as she brushed her hair. She wasn't going to force herself to wear a tight confining brassiere to bed, she swore as she watched her big breasts dance and gambol about underneath the material of her gown.

Suddenly, she felt a chill run down her spine. What was causing her to think this way? It was almost as if she was being taken over by some evil, menacing presence. Unexpectedly, she felt her nipples harden as they rubbed against the soft flannel of her nightgown.

This is silly, she smirked. This wasn't some horror movie. This was just her and her son being caught in a storm and having to share a room. That was all and that was all she was going to let it be. Shivering for some unknown reason, she hurriedly grabbed up her dirty clothes and quickly opened the door.

Stepping out into the room, she felt a rush of relief as she saw that he was standing by the television watching it.

See, she told herself, nothing is going on. He is just standing there watching television. There wasn't any depraved evil lurking in the room.

"Hi," Danny said, turning and looking over at her.

"Hi," she smiled back at him, still unable to shake the weird feeling.

"Uh, are you okay?" he asked her.

"What, uh, sure, uh, why do you ask?" she asked self-consciously as she padded over to the bed in her bare feet.

"You just look, uh, worried or something," he told her.

"Oh, nothing," she told him as she opened her suitcase.

Then as she started to drop her clothes into the suitcase, she noticed her panties lying on top of her other clothes.

She didn't remember leaving them like that when she had gotten her gown out. But maybe she had. She was tired.

Maybe that was it. She was so tired, her mind was playing tricks on her.

Stop it, she told herself, shoving her clothes down into the suitcase and slamming it shut.

"Uh, are you through, uh in the, uh, bathroom," Danny muttered, blushing brightly.

"Huh, oh, yeah, go ahead, I'm through," she told him.

"Okay," he told her, quickly heading for it.

What had come over her, she wondered as she spread the covers back. She was as jittery as a virgin at a high school prom. You're acting silly. So stop it, she told herself slipping under the covers. Then she flicked off the light and lay watching television.

She could still hear the shower running over the sound of the television. Then, she found herself wondering what Danny would look like naked.

"JUST STOP IT!" she groaned out loud as she heard the shower stop.

Gulping down the last of her wine, she lay under the covers waiting for Danny to join her in bed. But as she waited, she felt her eyelids growing heavier and heavier . . .

Slowly opening her eyes, she realized that she must have fallen to sleep. Now the room was room was pitch black and there was no comforting hum of the heater. As she lay there, she became aware of the sound of Danny breathing on his side of the bed.

After a few more moments, it dawned on her that the room was quite cool.

What now, she asked herself, slipping out from underneath the covers. Fumbling around for her purse, she finally found it and snapped it open. Digging around inside it, she pulled out the penlight she kept there. Shuffling over to the thermostat, she shined the feeble little light on it.

My goodness, she thought when she saw that the temperature was only thirty degrees. Tapping the thermostat, she saw that it was set on eighty. The heater was apparently not working. Tapping it a couple more times, she waited for it to come on, but nothing happened. Stepping over to the window, she peered out into the darkness and saw that there were no lights on anywhere.

The storm must have knocked out the power, she thought, stumbling over to the closet. Feeling on the shelf, she didn't find any extra blankets. Hurrying back over to the bed, she sat down on the edge and picked up the phone receiver. There wasn't even a dial tone. The storm had obviously done a number on them and knocked out all the power. Shivering in the cold, she turned off her penlight and quickly slipped under the covers again.

Wondering how long the power would be off, she hoped that it wouldn't be long because the room was growing colder by the moment.

"Mom?" she heard her son ask her.

"Yes, Honey," she answered him.

"I'm cold," he complained.

"I know, Dear, but the power is off and we don't have any heat," she mumbled, wondering what she else she could do.

"I hope that we don't freeze to death," Danny whimpered as his teeth began to chatter.

"We won't," she tried to reassure him, wondering how they would survive if the heat didn't come back on. Maybe they would have to go to the car with its heater, she thought, hoping that it wouldn't come to that.

"My ears are cold," he whined.

"Put your head under the covers," she told him.

What else could they do to stay warm, she wondered? They didn't seem to have a lot of choices.

They could cuddle up together and keep each other warm with their own body heat, she thought, forgetting her earlier misgivings about sleeping with her son. This was an emergency.

"Scoot over here and we can try to keep each other warm," she told him, holding up the covers so he could slide up next to her."

"Uh, Okay," she heard him say, his voice muffled by the covers as he slipped under them.

Hoping that she was doing the right thing, she felt the bed lurch as her son scooted over next to her.

Her mind was in turmoil as she felt her son snuggle up against her. Wondering what she had gotten them into, she could hear his teeth chattering as his whole body shivered.

Drastic times call for drastic solutions, she told herself as she pulled him into her body.

"Is that better?" she asked him.

"My ears are so cold they're burning," he whined.

Turning toward him, she cupped her hands over his ears and pulled his face into her soft, warm bosom. Thank goodness she had worn her flannel gown, she thought as she felt him slowly put his arms around her and gently, but purposefully, press his body up next to hers.

"Brrrrrrr," he shivered as he flattened himself against her, "my hands are like ice."

"I'm sorry, Baby," she apologized to him, "I wish I hadn't gotten us into such a mess."

"It's okay, Mother," Danny said. "At least we've got each other to keep warm."

"Yes, we do," she whispered, not knowing what else to say.

Her own hands were growing cold, too as the temperature in the room continued to plummet.

Danny was still shivering as they lay plastered up against each other.

How could she help him get warm, she asked herself?

The only way she could think was to use her own body heat. The bedding material wasn't enough to keep out the cold as it grew colder and colder.

Finally, she reached up and slowly unbuttoned the front of her gown.

"What are you doing, Mother?" she heard Danny ask as she slowly spread her gown open.

"Put your hands inside my gown," she whispered to him, "and warm your hands."

Shocked by her suggestion, he didn't respond for several moments.

"It's okay, baby," she told him, reaching down and taking hold of his hands.

"It's just to warm up your hands," she said, bringing his hands up to the opening.

He was in a daze. There was a roaring sound inside his head as he hesitantly eased his hands down into the gown. Fumbling clumsily, he suddenly found his hands cupped around his mother's big, round breasts.

"Oh, God," he groaned as he pressed his hands against the warmness of the soft flesh.

She didn't move or say anything as she felt him shyly exploring the warm roundness of her breasts.

Knowing what must be swirling through his head, she guided his hands down between her soft, drooping breasts.

She didn't want him to find her nipples with his fingers. She didn't want him to know that her nipples had swollen up so hard that they ached.

"Oh, Mother," he gushed, feeling the softness of her breasts collapse down around his hands, "your, uh, you are so warm and soft."

Putting her hands back on his ears, she pulled him to her tighter.

As they lay pressed together so tightly, sharing their body heat, she felt his shivering slowly taper off. Then after several minutes, he stopped shaking all together.

Just then, out of the darkness, she heard the wonderful sound of the heater shudder back to life. Thank goodness, she thought to herself. At least we won't freeze to death.

Even though she could feel a draft of warm air gently flowing across the bed, she knew it would be a long time before the temperature of the room would reach something close to comfortable.

Not knowing how long the heater would stay on, she let Danny keep his hands inside her gown.

She knew that it was probably wrong, but she let him keep his hands buried in between her breasts. But it was almost like having him as a baby again as he lay pressed up against her. It was strangely comforting to feel her son's hands on her breasts. It seemed to have a calming effect on both of them as the temperature began to slowly rise. She could no longer see her breath as the hum of the heater continued. Then she felt her eyelids growing heavier and heavier . . .

She didn't know how long she slept this time, but when she woke, she found the room ominously quiet once again.

While the heater wasn't on, the temperature of the room was comfortably warm. Danny was still lying pressed up against her with his hands inside her gown and his hands resting on her breasts.

As she lay beside him listening to his steady, rhythmic breathing, she wondered if she shouldn't make him go back to his side of the bed now that the room was warm again. As she thought about moving, she could feel the room growing cooler. Had the power gone off again? Or was the heater just in between cycles? Deciding to wait, she would see if the heater came back on before she made him move.

Nestled under the blankets, lying next to her son and sharing his warmth, she once again found herself slowly drifting off to sleep . . .

She didn't know how long she had slept this time, but as she woke, she had a nagging sense that something was wrong.

This time the room was warm again. She couldn't hear the heater running, but the room felt almost too warm.

Danny was still lying next to her, but she didn't feel his hands between her breasts any more. Why had he moved his hands out from between her breasts?

Then, almost at the same instant, she felt something slowly crawling down over her belly.

Still groggy from sleep, it took a while for her to realize that it was Danny's hand creeping down over her belly.

Shocked, she couldn't move as she felt her son's hot fingers slowly working their way down toward her womanhood.

She was mortified as she lay beside him paralyzed by shock and outrage.

How could he be doing this, she asked herself as she felt his fingers delicately brush over the curly hair covering her mons?

Do something, she told herself. Do something to stop him she groaned inwardly as she felt his fingers inch closer and closer to her secrecy.

Barely able to breathe, she became aware of a bulging hardness digging into her thigh.

DANNY HAD AN ERECTION! Her mind screamed at her. Her son's penis was hard and he had it shoved up against her leg while he groped her with his hand.

What could she do to stop this atrocity?

Still paralyzed with confusion and bewilderment. She couldn't move.

She lay there listening to him breathing heavily as he insistently pressed his manhood into her thigh. She couldn't believe that this was happening to her. How could she have been so stupid to let things get this far out of hand, she demanded?

Hoping that he was asleep and acting out a dream, she didn't move. But as she felt Danny's fingers probing closer and closer to her most sacred of places, she realized that his hand was touching her bare flesh. Her gown was unbuttoned and spread apart all the way down to her ankles.

How long had he worked to get that done as she had slept, she dizzily wondered?

She was lying on her back and her body was exposed from her neck all the way to her feet. She felt like she was totally vulnerable as she lay next to her son letting him grope her nakedness. The horror of it all came to her with such suddenness, it was like diving into an icy pool.

The shock too much. But, still she didn't move. Why, she didn't know. She knew what was happening, but she was afraid to stop it.

Then his finger brushed over her clitoris and she felt a slashing jolt of fright tear into her brain.

My God, she thought feverishly, he already knows how to excite a woman.

Then with her mind in such commotion, she shuddered slightly as she felt her body respond to this unsolicited attention. It was impossible to believe that this was happening.

She knew she had to stop him. And yet, her arms were weighted down on the bed my tons of cement, unable to move.

Suddenly, she felt a wave of disgust wash over her as she felt her instinctive sexuality beginning to assert itself. She was aghast to feel herself growing wet in response to her son's disastrous fumbling.

While she was aghast at her son's actions, she was even more appalled by her own lack of protest. The whole thing was preposterous. It couldn't be happening.

Maybe she was just having a terrible nightmare, she reasoned.

Then as Danny touched her clitoris again and delicately began fondling the swollen little bud with his finger, she knew that it was no dream. Even though she was sickened by what he was doing, she felt a tingle of physical pleasure tear up her spine and burst inside her brain. How could she be feeling aroused by his youthful blunderings when she knew she should be repulsed them, she wondered?

She knew that she had ignored her own sexual needs for much too long, but that was no excuse for this. She hadn't had a man since Danny's father had died, she told herself. There had been plenty of men who had asked her out, but she had turned them down. It had been six long years that she had chosen to forgo sex and devote herself to raising

Danny in the right way.

And now. Now, this was the way he repaid her.

She had devoted her life to her son and now he was defiling her in the most despicable way he could.

But how could he know how much she had sacrificed? But even then, even if he knew, there was no excuse for what he was doing. No son should ever do this to his own mother. Never, ever in a million years.

Still, even as part of her brain screamed at her to stop it all, she knew that he wasn't doing this to disgrace her. The hormones coursing through his blood stream had to be causing it. Danny was too good a son to do what he was doing. He must be suffering from some type of hormonal deficiency that would make act in such a heinous manner.

Even as she tried to excuse her son's actions, another part of her brain had surrendered to the sexual excitement he was touching off down between her legs.

This part of her brain controlled her instinctual response to sexual stimulation and was in charge of preparing her body for sex. She couldn't stop her body from reacting, no matter who was causing it to happen.

It was inborn to react and she was responding as any woman would, even though the advances were inappropriate, perverse and disgusting. This part of her brain wasn't capable of distinguishing right from wrong and was simply preparing her body for sex. It didn't care with whom.

Yet another part of her felt a perverted arrogance, knowing that her son found her physically attractive. It was bizarrely romantic in a grotesque kind of way, she drunkenly thought. Not in the romantic way of being seduced by a lover, but in a sick and deviant way.

Maybe down deep, deep inside every mother's soul, there was a tiny, minuscule grain of perversion. A perversion that could mutate into incestuous desire if exposed to the right circumstances. Regardless of what had caused it, she felt shocked to feel her revulsion weakening.

But still, she couldn't let it happen. There was no excuse for what they were doing. Suddenly, she realized that by saying they, she had included herself in the perversion. As if she was capitulating to the travesty.

And yes, she still felt a degenerate egotism that he found her attractive. For some reason, she found that in a grotesque, crazy manner, it was insanely exciting that he found her sexually attractive. Even knowing that it was depraved and hideously wrong.

The wickedness of it all was pushing any sense of propriety from her mind. The long years of abstinence had built up such forces, there was nothing that could hold back those unfilled needs now.

He had unwittingly lit the fuse to a bomb, setting up an explosion that could rock them both and send them hurtling into oblivion.

With each passing second, Susan found the whole thing more perversely exciting and insanely wicked. It was like returning to her childhood and playing doctor with the boy next door, except the boy was now her son. That made it even more depraved.

Then jealousy, the last element of her demise took hold of her. While it was horribly wrong, she wondered if she was the first woman he had touched. In some sick, distorted way, she felt an insane jealousy, hoping that she was the first.

While the warring factions of her mind fought for control, she felt his hot, bare skin pressing against her own bare skin. It suddenly dawned on her that he was naked too. When had he taken his pajamas off, she asked herself, shocked again by his boldness?

Then as he continued to fondle and toy with her tingling clitoris, his thrusting penis told her that he was becoming more and more aroused.

Still, a part of her screamed out for her to move away from him and stop the insane game.

The feelings and emotions swirling through her frantic brain were making her dizzy, incapable of logical thought.

Then almost in slow motion, she felt him slowly drape one leg over hers and gently began to press the granite hardness of his maleness into her thigh with growing insistence.

As the hard, firmness of his maleness dug into her thigh, she felt her pussy began leaking out more and more juice in anticipation of the final act of her violation.

Then, fatally, she realized that knowing she hadn't been able to stop it up to this point, she knew she wouldn't stop him now. She wouldn't be able to stop him from completing the final act of horror.

While she should have been thinking of a way to stop him, she perversely found herself wondering what he would feel like inside her. It had been six years since she had had a man inside of her body.

How big was he, she vulgarly wondered?

It felt like his manhood was huge as he pressed it against her. Maybe it was the sheer wickedness of her complicity in her own defilement that was distorting reality and making it seem even larger than it was.

She could almost feel him gathering himself for the final indignity as he insistently pulled on her leg with his. Like a gathering storm, she could sense his excitement and passion growing unchecked.

He was fully capable of mounting her, both physically and mentally at any moment, she groaned to herself.

A stabbing pang of sorrow tore though her mind as she found herself involuntarily spreading her legs apart, helping prepare herself for his invasion. Part of her screamed out for her to stop, but she couldn't keep her legs from slowly spreading apart wider and wider.

She was now compliantly accepting her fate and waiting for him to mount her. To mount her like some animal. Mount her and take her as his own. Mount her and fill her waiting emptiness with his toxic seed.

As her legs crept farther and farther apart, she heard his breathing growing raspy with desire. Still his leg pulled at her as he asthmatically gasped and wheezed.

Then she felt him jump as the furnace clicked on again.

She didn't move. Lying still, she felt the faint draft of warm air brush across her face.

Maybe he would stop, she prayed. Maybe he had come to his senses, she hoped, but after a few moments, she felt Danny resume pulling at her leg,

Finally, he stopped pulling at her leg. She felt him move his hand down away from her throbbing clitoris as he began to explore the slippery wetness of her exposed femininity.

She waited on, resigned to her fate as he ever so delicately probed her weeping womanhood with his fingers.

Even as hard as he was, she felt his cock lurch and harden even more as his fingers touched the waiting warmth of her cunt.

Then after a few moments, he moved his hand away from her wetness.

Now what? Was this it, she wondered as she felt him struggle up to his hands and knees.

Standing on his hands and knees with one leg straddling her leg, he waited for several moments almost as if he were waiting for her to stop him. Then when she didn't move, he slowly, but deliberately lifted his other leg over hers. Putting it down between her legs, he stood poised above her for several more moments.

Lewdly, she wished she could see what his manhood looked like as jutted out above her drooling pussy.

At last, the final act of defamation began as she felt him slowly lowering himself down toward her waiting motherhood. If she stopped him now, maybe they could salvage something of their life, she vaguely thought. But she knew she couldn't and made no effort to do so.

Then she felt his gigantic round cockhead touch her. It was like being touched by a red-hot poker and she couldn't stop herself from recoiling in shock and revulsion.

"SOOORRRYYYMOOTHHERRR," she heard him son gasp when she flinched.

But even as he was apologizing, he thrust himself down at her and his ripe, hardness quickly sliced down into the dripping wetness of her vagina.

Then, with a grunt, he drove himself down into her and in less than a heartbeat, he had buried half of his monstrous penis inside of her burning slit before she could react.

"OH MY GAAAWWWDDDDdddd," she gasped as she felt his penis slice into her aching pussy.

"I'm so sorry, mother," he groaned, starting to pull himself back out of her.

"No put it in all the way," she heard her voice say as she shuddered, reaching around him and digging her fingernails into the cheeks of his ass to pull him into her.

"OHMYFUCKINGGOD," she shivered as she felt his iron-hard maleness slice deeper and deeper into her pussy.

"IT'S HUGE," she blurted out as she felt her emptiness being filled by his enormous cock.

She couldn't believe how big he felt when at last the hair-encircled base of his cock slammed into her thick bush. It was like having a great, hot telephone pole shoved inside of her. How could he be so big, she pondered as she felt him start to sob.

"Don't cry, Baby," she cooed, lifting her long, lovely legs up and dropping her heels down onto his butt, "do it to me. Do it like you wanted to. Do it to Mommy."

Sounding like a wounded buffalo wheezing and snorting, he pulled his cock back and suddenly began to fuck her with deep, hard strokes.

Within moments, he was pounding his cock into her so hard, the whole bed was rattling and creaking as if it were about to collapse. She had never been so physically violated. His giant penis was stretching her pussy to its very limits, threatening to tear her apart with each appalling, slashing thrust.

Her mind was in such turmoil, she didn't know if she would be able to survive with her sanity. His colossal penis was so gigantic, it was almost like giving birth to him once again as he stretched her tight, clenching vagina to its limit.

But as he deliriously flung himself at her time after time, she knew that he couldn't last long. The overwhelming passion and depravity of their incestuous coupling were too exciting for him to withstand and within seconds she felt him losing control.

The violence of his ravaging attack was so brutal, she felt battered, both inside and outside even though it had only lasted for seconds . But when he began to scream out his rage and drove his cock into her with one final savage thrust, she felt her own orgasm burst to life and fill her soul with pleasure.

It felt as she was being consumed by some wicked raging fire of love and hate as her pussy collapsed down around her son's cock, imprisoning it inside of her.

Then, all at once, the monster imprisoned inside of her began to explode, jerking and spewing out its malevolence deep inside of her.

As she was being rocketed to heights of erotic pleasure she had only dreamed of before, she felt her son's beautiful, gigantic penis erupting inside of her like a great, overheated volcano spurting out its fiery load into her scorched pussy.

Indulging herself in a heinous pleasure that was so deep it was almost transcendental, she felt herself become divorced from her body.

While her body writhed and thrashed about underneath her son, she seemed to float above it. Even though her mind was being pounded by titanic waves of perverse delight, she could still feel her son's great malignant cannon jerking and shuddering inside of her.

Within moments, he had filled her to the point of overflowing with his rich, creamy cream, but still the great fleshy weapon discharged over and over again. The force behind the ejaculations was so great, she could feel the meaty channel of her cunt stretching and expanding until it seemed it would burst. When her cunt had collapsed down around her son's enormous cock, it had formed such a tight seal none of his thick purulent semen could escape out of her over-stuffed pussy. With her pussy plugged by her son's gigantic cock, the repeated eruption of his cock was pumping more and more thick, hot cum into her as the pressure inside of it grew and grew. Each time it did, she felt her pussy expand and distort as it became fuller and fuller of his rich, creamy semen. She had never felt anything like it, but still his gargantuan prick continued to spurt and spurt geyser after geyser of his thick, hot cream into her.

Even as the pressure inside her cunt continued to grow, her orgasm went on and on until it seemed like it was going to last forever. Torrents of pure wicked pleasure poured through her mind endlessly, filling her with such passion, she didn't want it to ever stop.

But at last, she felt the pleasure of her orgasm fading into a dull, pulsing glow of satisfaction.

Even though she felt like she had been orgasming for hours, she could still feel her son's impressive cock still firing off. As depraved and evil as their act of incestuous copulation was, she felt driven to take every last droop of her son's seed-laden silt as she gently forced him into her by digging her heels into his buttocks.

Lying atop her, grunting and groaning as he thrust himself into her, he couldn't stop it from erupting inside the hot, sucking hole between her legs.

She didn't think he would ever stop coming as the pressure inside her cunt continued to build and build to an almost unbearable level.

Then finally, with one last wheezing grunt, he shoved his mammoth prick into her as deeply as he could for one last gigantic discharge.

Never had she been penetrated so deeply by any man. Not even Danny's father. She knew that with certainty as she felt his mammoth prick jerk violently and spew out another tremendous gusher of cum. It was a colossal gusher of cum and it brought the pressure inside of her to the bursting point.

As the final gusher of his hot, creamy cum spurted inside of her, she knew it was too much for her brimming pussy. Suddenly, she felt the overwhelming pressure of the trapped cum break the seal around the giant cock. The instant the bond was broke, a great gusher of his viscid, thick cum spurted out of her cunt and splashed down his legs coating them with its hot stickiness. But, even after the first titanic wave of cum had escaped from her cunt, the flow continued like a severed artery, sending pulsating gushes of his hot cum spewing out of her cunt and running down the crack of her ass onto the bed.

After several seconds, as her cunt leaked out his offering, he groaned and collapsed down on top of her.

After he hadn't moved for a few seconds, she knew that he was finally through with her.

Lying on her back with her legs drawn up and her feet in the air, she slowly let her legs down to the bed. Although he only weighed a little over a hundred-fifty pounds, he was dead weight and she could scarcely breathe. Straining, she gently rolled him over onto his side beside her. As she did, she winced as his cock, still impressively thick and heavy, flopped out of her abused pussy. She had thought he was asleep, but as she turned toward him, she heard hear him weeping softly.

Suddenly, the anger and condemnation she had been feeling turned to sympathy for some reason. She felt as if she had betrayed him . . . and her all at the same time.

"Don't cry," she whispered softly, pulling him to her and wrapping her arms around him drawing his face down into her naked bosom, "what's done is done. We can't undo it."

"Oh, Mom, I'm so sorry," he blubbered.

She could feel the wetness of his tears on her breasts as he wept, but she didn't know what to do to comfort him. There was nothing she could do to erase the horrible sin he had just inflicted upon her.

She knew that it was just one of life's terrible tragedies that they would have to somehow learn to live with.

Holding him tightly against her nakedness, she waited for him to stop crying. Luckily, the heater continued to blow out warm air, as they lay uncovered, pressing their naked bodies together. Neither of them spoke for the longest time until Danny's sobs grew quieter and quieter until they finally stopped.

Still holding him clutched against her body, she looked down at him. Seeing that his breathing was regular and deep, she eased back away from him and saw that he had cried himself to sleep. Trying not to wake him, she gently rolled him away from her. He stirred momentarily and mumbled something intelligible, but quickly went back to sleep.

She carefully scooted over to the edge of the bed and slowly got up. As if to remind her of their wickedness, she felt a gusher of thick, syrupy cum gush out of her pussy and lewdly trickle down her leg. Hurrying into the bathroom, she closed the door and flicked on the light.

Standing there, she looked down at herself and with perverted fascination watched her son's thick, potency slowly ooze out of her to run down her legs, coating her inner thighs with the evidence of his virility. Then bending over to see if she was still leaking, she felt her gown slip off her shoulders and fall uselessly to the floor. Bending over, she picked it up and stuffed it up between her legs hoping to check the river of thick, potent cum that was still flowing from her pussy.

Feeling miserably betrayed, defiled, guilty, sated, and yet somehow fulfilled all at the same time, she shuffled out of the bathroom and over to the window.

Glancing down at her watch, she saw that it was three o'clock in the morning as she opened the blinds and looked out onto the white snowscape outside. She felt so lonely and used, it seemed like she was the only person in the world.

What a fool she was, she thought as she peered out into the night.

The intensity of the storm outside seemed almost a match for the maelstrom swirling around inside her head. And neither storm was giving any indication that it would let up any time soon.

The storm outside was definitely not diminishing in strength. If anything, it appeared to be getting worse. It looked like they were trapped inside their self-inflicted prison as the drifting, wind-blown snow piled against the door was at least two feet deep and getting deeper. It looked there would be no quick escape from their incarceration. They would have to face each other and probably spend the rest of the day in close quarters, held hostage by the storm.

Watching the snow swirl and whorl about, she felt as if she was trapped in a nightmarish fantasy dream. But it was definitely not a dream, she thought as she felt the manifestation of its reality starting to dry and itch as it coated her inner thighs. This night should never have happened in a million years, she told herself. But now that it had, she had to find a way to get past it without losing her sanity.

After staring out into the night for several minutes, she finally crept back into the bathroom. Standing there, she stared at her reflection in the mirror. How could she have let this happen, she asked herself again and again. She had, had so many opportunities to stop it, but she hadn't. There was no answer as she splashed water on her face trying to rinse away the guilt along with the tears that were trickling down her cheeks. Sobbing quietly, she watched her big naked breasts mockingly wiggle and jiggle. But then as she softly wept, she suddenly felt a sense of calm wash over her.

It was done and she couldn't turn back the clock, she thought as she slowly dried her face. What was done was done. Now what would the future hold? This was the important thing.

Wetting a washcloth, she bent over and slowly wiped at the sticky coating of drying semen that covered her inner thighs. After several minutes, she had cleaned most of it off. But even as she washed it away, more of it still dribbled out of her aching pussy. Giving up, she dried herself and stuffed a hand towel between her legs to soak up the rest that dribbled out.

Standing before the mirror looking at her reflection, she realized that the world hadn't come to an end. She was still a beautiful woman even if she had sinned grievously. It had been a catastrophic calamity, but life would go on and she would still have to face reality with her son, no matter what. Finally, she stood up straight and pulled her shoulders back. Thrusting her heavy, pendulous breasts out, she turned and walked out of the bathroom.

The bathroom light bathed the room in a soft glow as she quietly tiptoed back to the bed. Danny was still asleep, lying just as she had left him. Sitting down on the edge of the bed, she felt a little better now that she had faced the demons that haunted her.

Looking down at her sleeping son, she was initially disgusted with herself to find her eyes drawn to his penis. She had only fooled herself, she realized. She hadn't come to terms with it at all and now she felt a sudden sense of shame as she gawked at his exposed manhood. No matter how evil it was, she couldn't stop herself from feeling a sudden tingle of perverse excitement remembering what the monster had felt like inside of her.

Mentally, she felt as she had taken a beating at the hands of her son. His attack had been a horrific blow to her psyche, but despite herself, she had perversely derived pleasure from the physical side of the attack.

Before tonight, she had successfully been able to put sex aside. She had almost forgotten what it felt like to have a man inside her. Despite her abhorrence of what he had done to her, she knew that he had awakened feelings inside of her that had been best left alone. But now the hunger was back and needed to be satisfied once again.

Just thinking about having him inside of her caused a vulgar warmth to spread out from the throbbing core of her womanhood. Trying to fight off the feeling of need, she sat unmoving for several minutes, just watching the slow rise and fall of her son's chest. As she looked at him, she felt the need to have him inside of her again.

While she still loved him as a mother, it was all different now. It wasn't the pure, unselfish love of mother for her son. The new love had mutated into a melding of maternal and erotic love. She didn't know how she could go from hating him one moment to, to this. How could she even think it? Then suddenly she felt a glowing ember of desire spark to life down deep inside her soul. It was beyond her comprehension. How could she be having such evil thoughts about her son? This was her baby that she was thinking about. How could she hunger for him with such passion? How could she ever forgive herself for what she was thinking, she wondered out loud as she slowly reached down and gently touched his sleeping manhood?

Staring at his thick, bloated maleness made her almost giddy with need. As disgusting and depraved as it was, she had to have it inside of her again.

Studying the monstrosity, she couldn't believe that the evil, sleeping giant could belong to her son. It was almost as if Satan had taken the form of her son and had grown a huge cock to mock her . . . or to please her? No man, much less a boy, and even less, her son could possess such a fiendish monstrosity. Holding the demonic monster in her hand, she saw that even in its soft state, it was at least six inches long. It was no wonder she had felt stretched out of shape by the huge appendage. He had felt so huge when he was hard, it had felt like he was able to fit inside her. But probably part of the size of his cock was distorted by the sheer depravity of the act.

It seemed as if Danny had morphed into two separate entities. The one being her loving, caring son and the other, this man. This man with this, this thing down between his legs.

Looking down at the great, swollen man-thing, she wondered how much bigger it would get when he was hard. She had felt its size, but she wanted to see it this time. Compelled by desire, she knew that she must find out. But knowing that if she did, teasing a monster of such unholy origins would only lead to another defilement, she slowly began to gently stroke it as it flopped flop about lifelessly. It felt like it weighed ten pounds, she feverishly thought as she gently squeezed and fondled it.

To her disappointment, nothing happened for several long moments. Then gradually, like a waking giant, it slowly began to swell and stiffen. Gently, she rolled her son over onto his back and took hold of him with both hands as he stirred and groaned. Stopping for a moment, she waited until his breathing returned to normal before she began to worry and tease the malignancy once again.

Lovingly coaxing her son's slumbering penis back to hardness, she watched on with lecherous pride as it sluggishly struggled to regain its former malevolence. Bewildered, she couldn't believe that a teenage boy could be so big. Especially her own baby boy. How could her baby have such a prick unless he was possessed, she asked herself? Feeling his monstrous penis growing harder and harder in her hand, she knew it was no dream or nightmare either. This was reality.

Amazed that it was still growing bigger, she lustfully wondered how big it really was. Then suddenly she remembered making pom-poms for Danny's school during one of her charitable days. She also remembered that the strips of paper had to be six inches long. Wanting to hurry, she had measured her hand and it was six inches from her wrist to the tip of her middle finger.

Morbidly, she laid his elephantine penis down on his belly. The strange feeling of playing doctor with her neighbor once again came over her as she laid her hands on him. Putting her wrist at the base of his giant where it rose out of the almost hairless ball sac, she spread her hand up the length of his cock. Still, it only covered about two-thirds of his cock.

Then, she stood the great cylinder of granite hardness up and began to stroke it roughly. As she did, she watched Danny slowly stirring back to life as his eyes flickered open. She saw a momentary flicker of panic flash across in his flared eyes, but she didn't give him time to react. Quickly rising up on her hands and knees, she threw one long, shapely leg over him, straddling him with her oozing, weeping womanhood poised directly above his stiff, swollen man-thing.

A look of incredulity spread across his face when he looked up and found his mother's big, beautiful breast ponderously dangling above his face. He seemed too shocked to move but his eyes followed her hand with open-mouthed wonder as he watched her reach down between her splayed-out legs and grasp hold of his cock.

The suddenness of awaking to find his mother hovering above him and preparing to mount him was almost too much to take. He was having a difficult time trying not to erupt and spill his boiling load out into her hand as she held his cock up and seated its rounded tip in the opening of her drooling socket.

Feeling her son's cock lurch dangerously, she realized that he was so excited, he could erupt at any moment. Hurriedly, she held his great cock perpendicular to his body and squatted down, lowering her ripe, oozing woman-gash down toward it. Time seemed to stop until suddenly their bodies touched in the unholiest of ways, forcing both of them to groan with anticipation and excitement.

She couldn't believe how huge his hard, rubbery cock head felt as she forced herself down on him, straining to force her tight wetness down over the immense swollen hard roundness of his cockhead. Grunting with effort, she finally felt it begin to slip inside of her.

"Oh, Danny," she gushed as she felt the mammoth penis-head finally begin to penetrate

same time. Then with a sick and perverted arrogance, she wondered how many women could claim to have made love to the fruit of their loins. It was so evilly wicked, she felt herself shivering with depraved excitement.

Then, bending down and lowering one, great bulging nipple into her son's mouth, she slowly began to lift her hips, letting his giant, juice-slathered cock slither out of her. As Danny hungrily sucked on her big sensitive nipple, she felt another tiny pinch of pain as the swollen knob of his manhood slipped out of her cervix. She slowly lifted her hips higher and higher until at last, she finally stopped. Only the bloated ball of his penis-head remained inside the hot, dripping gash of her vagina as she straddled him standing on her hands and knees over him. Poised above him, her buttocks thrust into the air, she paused for a few moments, concentrating on the erotic sensations flowing from her nipple and cunt. Finally, with an unmotherly grunt, she thrust herself back down on her son's steel-like hardness, absorbing the entire thing back inside her pussy in one lightning thrust.

"Oh, FUCK," she gasped as their bellies slapped together lewdly.

"Unhhhhhffffkkkkk," Danny mumbled out around the breast-meat that was filling his mouth.

She felt his great weapon nudge up against her cervix again, but she could feel the channel of her cunt lengthening, adapting to it and no longer giving her any pain, only pleasure.

Grinding her pelvis down onto him, she sent his bloated cock twirling around inside the burning tightness of her overstuffed pussy.

After a few moments of savoring the wickedness, she began to slowly raise and lower her hips, forcing her son's gigantic man-thing in and out of her overheated cunt. It gave her such pleasure to feel his wonderful man-thing inside her, she tried to reason why it was sinful. In and out, in and out it went, stretching her tight, clenching pussy to its limit. Every time it created a vacuum inside of her as it exited with the saturated inside of her pussy wetly clinging to it. Even though she was stroking his cock ever so slowly, she could feel another cataclysmic orgasm building inside her.

Then suddenly, almost without warning, she found herself tottering on the verge of climaxing once again. But she wanted to prolong the heavenly anticipation that was pouring from her pulsating vagina. Hoping that it wouldn't trigger her climax, she slammed herself down on his jutting maleness, taking all of him inside of her again. Stopping, she lay atop him with his whole cock buried up inside of her. In her preoccupation with postponing her orgasm, she had jerked her breast away from her son. Now he lay looking up at her with such a look of love and wonder, she almost burst into tears.

Numbed by the intensity of her orgasm, she couldn't move for the longest time as she lay atop her son. Reveling in the feeling of total gratification, she could feel Danny's colossal cock ever so slowly shrinking and retreating back down the drenched channel of her vagina. But, even after fifteen minutes and she knew that he would not get any smaller, she knew he still had at least six inches of his cock imbedded inside of her.

Then, sleepily, she slowly sat up.

Seeing his mother rise, Danny looked up at her adoringly.

Smiling down at him, she reached around behind her. Feeling down to where they were still joined together, she gently lifted his wet, sticky balls in her hand. Rolling them and fondling them softly, she wondered how much of his thick, potent cream was left inside their great, round warmness.

Toying with his soft, heavy balls, she looked over at the window and saw that the snow had stopped. It was letting up, she realized. While she was tired now, and needed to sleep, she knew that before it was over, she would know how much potent cream her son had left over.

It didn't look like there would be any way they could leave any time soon, but with the snow stopping, she would just have to wait and see.

"Time for a break," she sighed, lifting herself up off him and letting his thick, heavy cum-coated cock slip out of her cunt.

"I think it's time we got some sleep," she mumbled lying down beside him and pulling the covers up over them.

"Night, Mom, I Love you," Danny said as he nestled up against her, pulling her to him.

"Night, My Love, I Love you, too, " she murmured drowsily looking down at her watch.

Seeing that it was just after three o'clock in the morning, she closed her eyes.

Lying there by her son, she was shocked at how normal it now felt. Funny but earlier she had been cursing the day and dreading tomorrow. Now she was looking forward to it and almost giddy about it. Bewildered by her sudden change of heart, she felt herself drifting off and was asleep within moments . . .

As she slept, she dreamed that she and Danny were walking through the snowstorm. They pushed through the snowdrifts, holding onto each other, getting their strength from the love that now seemed to flow between them. Suddenly she realized that neither of them wore any clothes, but amazingly they weren't cold. It was a strange, haunting dream with no rhyme or reason. They just kept walking through the snow, holding onto each other for the longest time. There didn't seem to be any point to the dream until all at once, they tripped and fell down in the snow, rolling over and over down a long hill.

Although the dream snow was cool to the touch, but it wasn't cold as they continued to roll down the hill. At last the ground leveled out and she finally stopped rolling. Lying on her back, she looked around to find Danny and saw him still rolling down the hill behind her. Then in slow motion, she watched as he lazily rolled one last time and came to rest on top of her looking down into her face. Looking up into his face, she felt such a love for him, it almost made her cry. While the love pouring out for him was the maternal love of a mother for her son, she once again became aware of their nakedness. Even though he was lying on top of her, he didn't seem to weigh anything as she ran her fingers through his long hair. Then to her astonishment, he leaned down and delicately kissed her nipples, letting his lips linger on each one for only a moment. Then as she was trying to comprehend the reason for their nakedness and why he would be kissing her breasts, she felt his manhood pressing into her belly, hard and big.

Lost in her dream world with her son, she watched on with disbelief as he got to his hands and knees. Staring down at his giant, jutting maleness, she looked on in dread as it slashed back and forth above her belly like a great, evil one-eyed snake searching for prey. As terrible and menacing as it was, she found a beauty in it as it hovered above her. Then, just as she started to reach out and touch it, she saw Danny slowly lower his hips and point the great, round head of his wicked snake at her waiting womanhood. How could he being doing this, she wondered with horror? But she did nothing to stop him. Didn't he know that she was his mother? And no son should ever make love to his mother?

Then he was inside her. Thrusting himself into her, his cock felt like a great, meaty sword as it sliced down into her hot pussy.

Suddenly, she awoke. It was no dream. Looking up, she saw Danny smiling down at her as he drove his great, swollen penis in and out of her pussy.

Shaking her head, trying to clear the remnants of the wickedly delightful dream from her head, she tried to push him away.

What in God's name was happening, she wondered, dazed and bewildered by his actions? Her mouth flew open in astonishment and she quickly looked down and saw that it was indeed her son's cock that was sliding into her pussy. Then just as she started to scream out her rage, everything came rushing back to her with the clarity of a cold shower.

"Mom, what's wrong?" she heard Danny ask her as he saw her eyes flare with fear and bewilderment, "Don't you love me anymore?"

"Oh, I'm sorry, Baby," she cooed, half closing her eyes and spreading her legs wider apart, "I just forgot for a second."

"Is it okay?" he asked her, pausing in mid stroke, holding himself half in and half out of her pussy. "Or do you not want to do it anymore?"

"Of, course Mommy wants to do it," she smiled up at him, reaching down and digging her nails into his buttocks as she pulled him into her, "I just forgot for a moment that you weren't only my son any more. Now you're my lover, too."

"Oh, Mom, it feels so good," he groaned as he quickly slid the rest of his swollen manhood into her hot, clenching pussy.

"Yes is does," she whispered to him, pushing herself against his thrust and taking the last inch of his monstrous cock into her pussy.

Within moments, Danny was slowly stroking his cock into her with deep, long, slow strokes. Each time he entered the deep, wet depths of her steaming gash, he drove himself in all the way to the hilt. In and out, in and out like a great chugging machine, he fucked her.

Reveling in the feel of her son's giant prick sliding in and out of her throbbing cunt, she looked over to the window and saw that the snow was no longer swirling outside.

"I think the storm is over," she murmured as she lay under Danny taking ever one of his hard, jarring penetrations and wanting more.

"I hope it isn't. I could stay like this with you forever, Mom," he grunted as he continued to drive his cock into her. Turning away from the window, Susan looked down between their bodies. Even though it was still snowing heavily, the light coming into the room was steadily growing brighter and brighter. She could now see her son's great, round pillar of cock-meat steadily sliding in and out of her dripping cunt as it glistened sickly in the dim light. Glistening with the juices of her pussy. Dripping with the juices of his own mother's cunt, she groaned to herself. Even as he hammered his cock into her, she glanced at her watch and saw that it was almost eight o'clock in the morning. While it was growing lighter outside, the sun's brightness was dimmed by the swirling snow.

What a way to start a day, she thought as she lay under her son watching his hugeness sliding in and out of her widely dilated vaginal opening. His gigantic cock was so big and round, she could feel it scraping her tingling clitoris every time he slammed it inside of her. This was quickly bringing her to another orgasm. Then ever so slightly, she felt the rhythm of his fucking pick up. She was unable to control her rampart emotions and felt herself slipping over the edge toward another orgasm. Looking up, the last thing she saw before she slipped into the soft, entombing wonder of her orgasm, was the light glistening of her son's brow as he was beginning to sweat from the exertion of fucking her.

As he continued to pound his penis into his mother's softness, he realized with a start that she was climaxing again as her body began to quiver and her eyes rolled back into her head. Even though she was tripping out again, he didn't stop as he drove his cock into her harder and harder. He could hear their wet genitals slapping together as his mother made weird, unintelligible noises. Still he fucked her as her body shook and writhed under him.

Now he could feel his own sap quickly rising and seeking an outlet.

His own eruption was imminent as he quickened the pace once again. Just as he moved his pace to another level, he felt his mother stop shaking and saw her eyes flicker open again.

Smiling up at her son, Susan slowly raised her feet up into the air, exposing her womanhood to him completely. Holding her feet up in the air and tilting her pelvis back she let him penetrate her to his limit with every stroke. Smiling up at him, she watched her feet swinging back and forth above him every time he rammed his enormous male-thing into her. Then reaching around her legs, she dug her long, pink fingernails into his ass again, goading him to fuck her even harder. He responded and was soon slamming his cock into her so hard, the bed was creaking and groaning in protest.

"Oh, Fuck, Oh, Fuck, Oh, Yes, Oh, Fuck, Oh, Yes, Oh, Fuck, Me, Yes, Fuck, Me, Oh, My, Fuck, God, I, Fuck, Love, It, Oh, Fuck, Oh, Yes, Oh, Fuck, I, Fuck, Love, You," Susan stammered out between the hammering blows her son was raining down on her defenseless cunt.

"Yeaunh, Yeaunh, Yeaunh, Yeaunh, Fuck, Yeaunh, Yeaunh, Yeaunh, Yeaunh," Danny grunted as he drove himself into her waiting heat. Faster and harder he drove himself, stroking her so deep, she felt like his cock would come out of her mouth at any moment. She couldn't believe it but she suddenly found herself tottering on the edge of another breathtaking orgasm, and just as she felt herself losing control, she felt her son's giant cannon explode inside of her.

"AAAAHHHHEEEEEEEESSSSSEEEIIITTTTTTT!" he screamed out as his cock jerked and sent a huge gusher of his thick, scalding cum spurting out onto the sensitive walls of her clenching pussy.

"AHHHHYYYeeeeSSSS," she groaned out in pure ecstasy as her body began to thrash about uncontrollably.

It was unbelievable. Her mind convulsed with the pleasure that was pouring up out of her pussy where her son's giant peter spurted and spurted. Nothing in the world existed except the two of them joined together in their unholy wedlock.

Her pussy clenched and milked his enormous man-thing, making it jerk and explode over and over again. Each time it exploded inside of her, she could feel a huge gusher of his white-hot cum spew out into her, filling her totally with his masculinity. Again and again, it happened, each time driving her deeper and deeper into the consuming depths of her orgasm until at last she fainted, her pleasure circuits all overloaded.

She didn't how long she had been out when she felt herself slowly floating back to life.

Suddenly, there was a knock on the door.

"ARE YOU FOLKS OKAY IN THERE?" she heard someone holler from outside the door.

Hung over and dazed by the intensity of her orgasm, she slowly realized that someone was knocking on their door.

Then as the stark reality of what had happened came rushing back to her, she realized that Danny was still lying on top of her. Then with a start, she felt his penis still inside of her.

"UH, UH, YES," she shouted out, hoping whoever it was wouldn't come inside and catch them.

"UH, UH, JUST A MINUTE," she sputtered, shaking Danny by the shoulder.

"Get off and hide under the covers," she hissed as he clumsily rolled off her.

Shoving Danny off her, she rolled away from him.

"Whut's goin on?" Danny snorted, as Susan struggled to get up, "what's going on, Mom?"

"Just shut up and stay under the covers," she whispered, throwing the covers over him, "there's someone at the door."

"WHAT," he gasped in fear, "did they see us?"

"I hope not," she muttered, "but the fucking curtain is open. Just be quiet."

"I'LL BE THERE IN JUST A MINUTE," she hollered in the direction of the door as she grabbed one of the blankets off the bed and wrapped it around her.

Stumbling over to the door, she fumbled with the lock for a few seconds before she finally got it unlocked.

"Yes, what is it?" she mumbled, opening the door and seeing the manager standing outside bundled up in his parka with a shovel in his hand.

"UH, I'm, uh, just checking on everyone," he told her, seeing that she was obviously naked except for the blanket wrapped around her, "are you and your, uh, boy, okay?"

"Uh, Why, yes, we're fine," she stammered, blushing brightly at the mention of Danny.

"Well, the electricity should stay on and looks like the storm is letting up," the manager told her, trying to peek inside the room, "ya'll can stay as long as you need to. So give me a call if you two need anything."

"Thank you," she smiled back at him as bravely as she could, "I was just taking a shower to warm up but I think we'll be fine. I'll call you if we need you. Thanks."

Closing the door, she leaned against it for several moments waiting to make sure he left.

Then she saw him walk by the window and stop.

Quickly stepping over to the window, she jerked the curtains closed as he peered inside.

Wondering if their heinous crime against nature had been observed, she peeked out the curtain to see the manager trudging across the parking lot.

"Did he see us?" Danny asked, sticking his head out of the covers and staring at his mother.

"We'll just have to wait and see," she muttered, "but in the meantime, get dressed, so if he comes back we can lie our way out of it."

Both of them dressed and waited, but no one returned. After a while, Susan gathered up her courage and headed for the manager's cabin.

After a few knowing smirks, the manager took her money.

"Well, you and you, uh, son, come on back to visit us again some time," he leered taking the key from her.

"We'll just do that," she laughed nervously as she slipped back out to the car where Danny sat waiting for her.

"Did he know?" Danny asked her breathlessly as she slipped into the car.

"The idiot thought we were lovers," she smiled and leaned over and gave him a kiss as the manager peeked out the window at them.

"Well, we are, aren't we?" Danny smiled at her, waving at the manager. "Now?"

"Why, I guess that we are . . ." she laughed, backing the car up and driving out onto the recently-plowed highway. "I guess we are . . ."

THE END

Share your thoughts with us.
Take a moment to tell us how we're doing. Your feedback really matters.

You can reach us by:
Email: *my777books@yahoo.com*

Search for other titles by Sophie MacDonald.